THE FAMOUS SHORT STORIES

FIVE AND A HALF-TERM ADVENTURE

*Plea
- thi

The Famous Five

Timmy   Anne   Dick   Julian   George

Text first published in Great Britain in Enid Blyton's Magazine Annual – No. 3, in 1956.
Also available in The Famous Five Short Stories, published by Hodder Children's Books.
First published in Great Britain in this edition in 2014 by Hodder Children's Books

8

A Catalogue record for this book is available from the British Library
ISBN 978 1 444 91625 6

Printed in China
Hodder Children's Books
A division of Hachette Children's Books
Hachette UK Limited, 338 Euston Road, London NW1 3BH

www.hachette.co.uk

Enid Blyton

FiVE AND A HALF-TERM ADVENTURE

illustrated by Jamie Littler

Hodder Children's Books

A division of Hachette Children's Books

Famous Five Colour Reads

For a complete list of the full-length
Famous Five adventures, turn to
the last page of this book

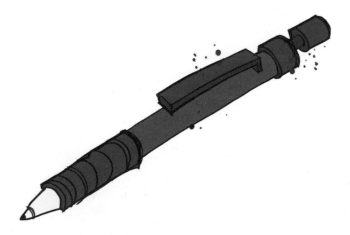

Contents

CHAPTER ONE

The **Five** were at Kirrin Cottage for a short half-term holiday. For once, both the boys' school and the girls' school had chosen the same weekend!

'It hardly ever happens that we can spend half-term together,' said Anne, fondling Timmy. 'And what luck to have such lovely weather at the beginning of November!'

'Four days off!' said George. 'What shall we do?'

'BATHE!' said Julian and Dick together.

'What!' said their aunt, horrified, **'Bathe in November! You must be mad! I can't allow that, Julian, really I can't.'**

'All right,' said Julian, grinning at his aunt. 'Don't worry. We haven't got our swim-suits here.'

'Let's walk over to Windy Hill,' said Dick. 'It's a grand walk, by the sea most of the way. And there may be blackberries and nuts still to find. I'd like a good walk.'

'**Woof,**' said Timmy at once, and put his big paw up on Dick's knee. He was always hoping to hear that magic word '***Walk!***'

'**Yes,** let's do that,' said Anne. 'Aunt Fanny, shall we take a picnic lunch – or it is too much bother to prepare?'

'Not if you help me,' said her aunt, getting up. 'Come along – we'll see what we can find. But remember that it gets dark **very** quickly in the afternoon now, so don't leave it too late when you turn back.'

CHAPTER TWO.

The Five set off half an hour later, with sandwiches and slices of fruit cakc in a knapsack carried by Julian. Dick had a basket for any nuts or blackberries. His aunt had promised a blackberry-and-apple pie if they did find any berries for picking.

Timmy was very happy. He trotted along with the others, sniffing here and there, and barking at a curled-up hedgehog in a hole in a bank.

'**Now, leave it alone,**' said George. 'You really should have learnt by now that **hedgehogs are not** meant to be carried **in your mouth, Timmy! Don't wake it up** – it's gone to sleep for the winter!'

'It's a heavenly day for the beginning of November,' said Anne. 'The trees still have their leaves – all colours: red, yellow, brown, pink – and the beeches are the colour of gold.'

'**Blackberries!**' said Dick, catching sight of a bush whose sprays were still covered with the black fruit. 'I say – taste them – they're as **sweet as sugar!**'

As soon as the blackberries were to be seen on bushes here and there, **the Five** slowed up considerably! The blackberries that were still left were big and full of sweetness.

'They **melt** in my mouth!' said
George. **'Try one, Timmy!'** But Timmy spat
the blackberry out in disgust.

'Manners, Timmy, manners!'
said Dick at once, and Timmy wagged his big
tail and pranced round joyfully.

It was a good walk but a slow one. They found a hazelnut copse and filled the basket with nuts that had fallen to the ground. Two red squirrels sat up in a nearby tree and chattered at them crossly. This was their nut copse!

'You can spare us a few!' called Anne. 'I expect you've got hundreds hidden away safely for the winter.'

They had their lunch on the top of **Windy Hill.** It was not a windy day, but, all the same, there was a good breeze on the top, and Julian decided to sit behind a big gorse bush for shelter. 'We'll be in the sun and out of the wind then,' he said. 'Spread out the lunch, Anne!'

'I feel **terribly hungry!'** said George. **'I can't** believe it's only just **one o'clock,** Julian.'

'Well, that's what my **watch** says,' said Julian, taking a sandwich. 'Ha – ham and lettuce together – just what I like. Get away, Tim – I can't eat with you trying to nibble my sandwich too.'

CHAPTER THREE

It was a magnificent view from the top of the hill. The four children munched their sandwiches and gazed down into the valley below. A town lay there, comfortably sprawled in the shelter of the hills. Smoke rose lazily from the chimneys.

'**Look** – there's a train running along the railway-line down there,' said George, waving her sandwich in its direction. 'It looks just like a toy one.'

'It's going to **Beckton,**' said Julian. 'See – there's the station – it's stopping there. It really does look like a **toy train!**'

'Now it's off again – on its way to **Kirrin,** I suppose,' said Dick. **'Any more sandwiches? What, none? Shame!** I'll have a slice of cake, then – hand over, Anne.'

They talked lazily, enjoying being together again. Timmy wandered from one to the other, getting a titbit here and a scrap of ham there.

'I think I can see another nut copse over yonder – the other side of the hill,' said George. 'I vote we go and see what nuts we can find – and then I suppose we ought to be thinking of going back home. The **sun is getting awfully low,** Ju.'

'**Yes, it is,** considering it's only about **two o'clock,'** said Julian, looking at the red November sun hardly showing above the horizon. 'Come on, then – let's get a few more nuts, and then go back home. I love that long path winding over the cliffs beside the sea.'

They all went off to the little copse, and to their delight, found a fine crop of hazelnuts there. Timmy nosed about in the grass and brought mouthfuls of the nuts to George.

'**Thanks, Timmy,'** said George. 'Very clever of you – but I wish you could tell the **bad ones** from the **good** ones!'

'**I say,**' said Dick, after a while, '**the sun's gone, and it's getting dark.** Julian, are you *sure* **your watch is right?**'

Julian looked at his watch. 'It says **just about two o'clock still,**' he said in surprise. '**Gosh** – I must have forgotten to wind it up or something. It's definitely **stopped** now – and it must have been **very** slow before!'

'Idiot,' said Dick. 'No wonder George thought it was long past lunchtime when you said it was one o'clock. We'll never get home before dark now – and we haven't any torches with us.'

'That cliff-path isn't too good to walk along in the dark, either,' said Anne. 'It goes so near the edge at times.'

29

'We'd better start back immediately,' said Julian. 'Awfully sorry about this – I never dreamed that my watch was wrong.'

'I tell you what would be a better idea,' said George. 'Why don't we just take the **path** down into **Beckton** and catch the **train** to **Kirrin?** We'll be so late if we walk back, and Mother will be ringing up the police about us!'

'Good idea of yours, George,' said Julian. **'Come on** – let's take the path while we can still see. It leads straight down to the town.'

CHAPTER FOUR

So away went **the Five** as fast as they could.
It was dark when they reached the town, but
that didn't matter, because the street lamps
were alight. They made their way to the station,
half-running down the main street.

'Look – there's **Robin Hood** on at the cinema here,' said Anne. 'Look at the **posters!**'

'And what's that on at the hall over there?' said George. **'Timmy, come here** – oh, he's shot across the road. **Come *HERE*, Timmy!'**

But Timmy was running up the steps of the Town Hall. Julian gave a sudden laugh. **'Look – there's a big dog show** on there – and old Timmy must have thought he ought to go in for it!'

'He smelt the dogs there,' said George, rather cross. **'Come on – let's get him,** or we'll lose the next train.'

The hall was plastered with posters of dogs of all kinds. Julian stopped to read them while George went in after Timmy.

'Some **jolly valuable dogs here,'** he said. 'Some beauties, too – look at the picture of this white poodle. Ah – here comes Tim again, looking very sorry for himself. I bet he knows he wouldn't win a single prize – **except for brains!'**

'It was the doggy smell that made him go to see what was on,' said George. 'He was awfully cross because they wouldn't let him in.'

'**Hurry up** – I think I can hear a **train coming!**' said Dick, and they all raced down the road to the station, which was quite near.

The train puffed in as they went
to the booking-office for their tickets.
The guard was blowing his whistle
and waving his flag as they rushed on
to the platform. Dick pulled open the
door of the very last compartment
and they all bundled in, panting.

'**Gosh** – **that was a near squeak,**'
said Dick, half-falling on to a seat. '**Look out,
Tim – you nearly had me over.**'

The four children got back their breath and looked round the carriage. It was not empty, as they had expected. Two other people were there, sitting at the opposite end, facing each other – a man and a woman. They looked at the **Five, annoyed.**

'**Oh,**' said Anne, seeing the woman carrying a shawled bundle in her arms, 'I hope we haven't **woken your baby.** We only just caught the train.'

The woman rocked the little thing in her arms, and crooned to it, covering its head with a shawl – a rather dirty one, Anne noticed.

'**Is she all right?**' asked the man. '**Cover her up more** – it's cold in here.'

'There, there now,' crooned the woman, pulling the shawl tighter. The children lost interest and began to talk. Timmy sat still by George, very bored. Then he suddenly sniffed round, and went over to the woman. He **leapt up** on to the seat beside her and **pawed** at the **shawl!**

CHAPTER FIVE

The woman shrieked and the man shouted at Timmy.

'Stop that! Get down!

Here, you kids, look after that great dog of yours. **It'll frighten the baby into fits!'**

'**Come here, Timmy,**' said George at once, surprised that he should be interested in a baby. Timmy whined and went to George, looking back at the woman. A tiny whimpering noise came from the shawl, and the woman frowned. '**You've waked her,**' she said, and began to talk to the man in a loud, harsh voice.

Timmy was **very disobedient!** Before George could stop him, he was up on the seat again, **pawing** at the woman and **whining.** The man **leapt up** furiously.

'**Don't hit my dog, don't hit him,** he'll **snap at you!**' shouted George – and mercifully, just at that moment the train drew in at a station.

'Let's get out and go into another carriage,' said Anne, and opened the door. The four of them, followed by a most unwilling Timmy, were soon getting into a compartment near the engine. George looked crossly at Timmy.

'Whatever came over you, Tim?' she said. **'You are never interested in babies!** Now sit down **and don't move!'**

Timmy was surprised at George's cross voice, and he crept under the seat and stayed there. The train came to a little station, where there was a small platform, and stopped to let a few people get out.

'It's **Seagreen Halt,**' said Dick, looking out. **'And there go the man and woman and baby** – I must say I wouldn't like them for a Mum and Dad!'

'It's quite dark now,' said George, looking through the window. 'It's a jolly good thing we just caught the train. Mother will be getting worried.'

CHAPTER SIX

It was nice to be in the cosy sitting-room at Kirrin Cottage again, eating an enormous tea and telling George's mother about their walk. She was very pleased with the nuts and blackberries. They told her about the man and woman and baby, too, and how funny Timmy had been, pawing at the shawl.

'He was *funny* **before** that,' said Anne, remembering. 'Aunt Fanny, there was a **dog show** on at **Beckton**, and Timmy must have read the posters, and thought he could go in for it – because he suddenly dashed across the road and into the **Town Hall** where the **show was being held!'**

'Really?' said her aunt, laughing. 'Well, perhaps he went to see if he could find the beautiful little white Pekinese that was **stolen** there **today!** Mrs Harris rang up and told me about it – there was such a to-do. The little dog, which was worth **£5,000**, was cuddled down in its basket one minute – and the next it **was gone!** Nobody was seen to take it, and though they hunted in every corner of the hall, there was no sign of the dog.'

'**Gracious!**' said Anne. '**What a mystery!** How could anyone possibly take a dog like that away **without being seen?**'

'Easy,' said Dick. 'Wrap it in a coat, or pop it into a shopping basket and cover it up. Then walk through the crowd and **out of the hall!**'

'**Or wrap it in a shawl** and **pretend** it was **a BABY** – like the little one in that dirty shawl in the train,' said Anne. 'I mean – we thought that was a baby, of course – but it could easily have been a dog – or a cat – or even a monkey. **We couldn't see its face!**'

There was a sudden silence. Everyone was staring at Anne and thinking hard. Julian **banged his hand on the table** and made everyone jump.

'There's something in what Anne has just said,' he said. 'Something worth thinking about!

Did anyone see even a glimpse of the baby's face – or hair? Did you, Anne – you were nearest?'

'**No,**' said Anne, quite startled. 'No, I didn't. I did try to see, because I like babies – but the shawl was pulled right over the face and head.'

'And I say – don't you remember how interested Timmy was in it?' said George, excited. '**He's never interested in babies** – but he kept on **jumping up** and **pawing** at the **shawl.**'

'And do you remember how the baby whimpered?' said Dick. 'It was much more like a **little dog** whining than a **baby,** now I come to think of it. No wonder Timmy was excited! He knew it was a dog by the **smell!**'

'**Whew!** I say – this is jolly exciting,' said Julian, getting up. 'I vote we go to **Seagreen Halt** and snoop round the tiny village there.'

CHAPTER SEVEN

'**No,**' said Aunt Fanny firmly. '**I will not
have that,** Julian. It's as dark as pitch outside,
and I don't want you snooping round for
dog-thieves on your half-term holiday.'

'Oh, I say!' said Julian, bitterly
disappointed.

'**Ring up the police**,' said his aunt.
'Tell them what you have just told me – they'll
be able to find out the truth very quickly.
They will be sure to know who has a baby
and who hasn't – they can go round snooping
quite safely!'

'All right,' said Julian,
sad to have a promising adventure
snatched away so quickly. He went to the
phone, frowning. Aunt Fanny might have let
him and Dick slip out to Seagreen in the
dark – it would have been such fun.

The police **were most** **interested** and asked a lot of questions. Julian told them all he knew, and everyone listened intently. Then Julian put down the receiver and turned to the others, looking quite cheerful again.

'They were jolly interested,' he said. 'And they're off to **Seagreen Village** straight away in the police car. They're going to let us know what they find. Aunt Fanny – **we CANNOT** go to **bed tonight** till we know what **happens!**'

'**No, we can't!**' cried all the others, and Timmy joined in with a bark, leaping round excitedly.

'Very well,' said Aunt Fanny, smiling. 'What a collection of children you are – you **can't even go for a** **walk** without **something happening!** Now – get out the cards and let's have a game.'

They played cards, with their ears listening for the ringing of the telephone bell. But it didn't ring. Supper time came and still it hadn't rung.

'It's no go, I suppose,' said Dick gloomily. 'We probably made a mistake.'

Timmy suddenly began to bark, and then ran to the door, pawing at it. **'Someone's coming,'** said George. **'Listen – it's a car!'** They all listened, and heard the car stop at the gate – then footsteps came up the path and the front-door bell rang. George was out in a trice, and opened it.

'Oh – it's the police!' she called. **'Come in,** do come in.'

CHAPTER EIGHT

A burly policeman came in, followed by another. The second one carried a bundle in a shawl! Timmy leapt up to it at once, whining!

'Oh! It **wasn't a baby,** then!' cried Anne, and the policeman smiled and shook his head. He pulled the shawl away – and there, fast asleep, was a **tiny white Pekinese**, its little snub nose tucked into the **shawl!**

'Oh – the darling!' said Anne.
'Wake up, you funny
little thing!'

'**It's been doped,**' said the policeman. 'I suppose they were afraid of it whining in the night and giving its hiding-place away!'

'Tell us what happened,' begged Dick. '**Get down, Timmy.** George, he's getting too excited – he wants the **Peke to play with him!**'

'Acting on your information we went to **Seagreen,**' said the policeman. 'We asked the porter what people got out of the train this evening, and if anyone carried a baby – and he said four people got out – and **two** of them were **a man and woman,** and the woman carried **a baby in a shawl.** He told us who they were – so away we went to the cottage . . .'

'**Woof,**' said Timmy interrupting, trying to get at the tiny dog again, but nobody took any notice of him.

'We looked through the back window of the cottage,' went on the policeman, 'and spotted what we wanted **at once!** The woman was giving the dog a drink of milk in a saucer – and she must have put some drug into it, because the little thing dropped down and fell asleep at once while we were watching.'

'So in we went, and that was that,' said the second policeman, smiling round. 'The couple were so scared that they blurted out everything – how someone had paid them to steal the dog, and how they had taken their own baby's shawl, wrapped round a cushion – and had stolen the dog quite easily when the judging of the Alsatians was going on. **They wrapped** the tiny dog in the **shawl,** just as you thought, and caught the **next train** home!'

'I wish I'd gone to **Seagreen Village**
with you,' said Julian. 'Do you know who
told the couple to steal the little dog?'

'Yes – we're off to **interview him now!**
He'll be most surprised to see us,' said the
burly policeman. 'We've informed the owner
that we've got her prize dog all right – but she
feels so upset about it she can't collect it till the

morning – so we wondered if you'd like to keep it for the night? Your Timmy can guard it, can't he?'

'Oh yes,' said George in delight. 'Oh, Mother – I'll take it to my room when I go to bed, and Timmy can guard the tiny thing as much as he likes. **He'll love it!'**

'Well – if your mother doesn't mind you having two dogs in your room, that's fine!' said the policeman, and signalled to the second one to give George the dog in the shawl. She took it gently, and Timmy leapt up again.

'No, Tim – be careful,' said George.

'Look what a tiny thing it is. **You're to guard it tonight.'**

Timmy looked at the little sleeping Pekinese, and then, very gently, he licked it with the tip of his pink tongue. This was the tiny dog he had smelt in the train, covered up in the shawl. Oh yes – Timmy had guessed at once!

'I don't know what your name is,' said Dick, stroking the small silky head. 'But I think I'll call you **Half-term Adventure,** though I don't know what that is in Pekinese!'

The two policemen laughed. 'Well, good night, Madam, good night, children,' said the burly one. 'Mrs. Fulton, the dog's owner, will call tomorrow morning for her Peke. He won a **£1,000 prize today** – so I dare say you'll get some of that for **a reward! Good night!'**

The **Five** didn't want a reward, of course – but Timmy had one for guarding the little Peke all night. It's on his neck – the **finest studded collar** he has ever had in his life! **Good old Timmy!**

If you enjoyed this Famous Five short story, there's plenty more action and adventure in the full-length Famous Five novels. Here is a list of all the titles, in the order they were first published.